There's a thief

"Please Dr. Berger," Mrs. Shelton said, "can you tell us about Jane Jansen? How is she? Did she have her baby?"

Dr. Berger smiled. "I was just with Mrs. Jansen," she said, "and she's doing very well. It will be a while before I can tell you any more than that."

Dr. Berger went to the coffee machine.

Cam, Eric, and Mrs. Shelton went back to their seats.

"It's your turn," Cam told Eric. "I said 'Naomi' and that ends with an 'I.'"

"Ian."

"Nellie."

"I'm getting a cup of coffee," Mrs. Shelton told Cam and Eric. "Are you thirsty? Would you like some juice?"

Cam and Eric wanted orange juice.

Mrs. Shelton looked on the couch. She lifted her coat. Then she lifted Cam's and Eric's coats. "Hey," she said. "Where's my purse?"

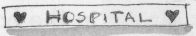

CAM JANSEN

CASE #25

The Valentine Baby Mystery

David A. Adler
Illustrated by Susanna Natti

PUFFIN BOOKS
An Imprint of Penguin Group (USA) Inc.

PUFFIN BOOKS

Published by the Penguin Group

Penguin Young Readers Group, 345 Hudson Street, New York, New York 10014, U.S.A.

Penguin Group (Canada), 90 Eglinton Avenue East, Suite 700,
Toronto, Ontario, Canada M4P 2Y3 (a division of Pearson Penguin Canada Inc.)

Penguin Books Ltd, 80 Strand, London WC2R 0RL, England

Penguin Ireland, 25 St Stephen's Green, Dublin 2, Ireland (a division of Penguin Books Ltd)

Penguin Group (Australia), 250 Camberwell Road, Camberwell, Victoria 3124, Australia
(a division of Pearson Australia Group Pty Ltd)

Penguin Books India Pvt Ltd, 11 Community Centre,
Panchsheel Park, New Delhi - 110 017, India

Penguin Group (NZ), 67 Apollo Drive, Rosedale, North Shore 0632, New Zealand
(a division of Pearson New Zealand Ltd)

Penguin Books (South Africa) (Pty) Ltd, 24 Sturdee Avenue,
Rosebank, Johannesburg 2196, South Africa

Registered Offices: Penguin Books Ltd, 80 Strand, London WC2R 0RL, England

First published in the United States of America by Viking,
a division of Penguin Young Readers Group, 2005
Published by Puffin Books, a division of Penguin Young Readers Group, 2006
This edition published by Puffin Books, a division of Penguin Young Readers Group, 2011

7 9 11 13 15 17 19 20 18 16 14 12 10 8

Text copyright © David A. Adler, 2005
Interior illustrations copyright © Susanna Natti, 2005
Logo illustration copyright © Penguin Young Readers Group, 2010
All rights reserved

CIP DATA IS AVAILABLE UPON REQUEST FROM THE LIBRARY OF CONGRESS

Puffin Books ISBN 0-14-240694-6

Set in New Baskerville

Printed in the United States of America

Kevi

Kevin Laes book

For Anne R. G.
with thanks
—D. A.

To Lydia
—S. N.

CHAPTER ONE

"Hey, look at this," Danny said.

Cam Jansen and her friends Eric and Beth looked.

Danny put a straw into his milk container. He blew milk bubbles that spilled onto the lunchroom table.

"That's not funny," Eric said.

"Well, this will be funny," Danny said.

His cream cheese and jelly sandwich, a large heart-shaped cookie, and an apple were on the table. Danny unwrapped the sandwich, took off the top piece of bread, and put it on his nose. It stuck.

Cam and Eric started talking about math. Their teacher, Ms. Benson, had just taught a lesson on different kinds of triangles. Beth ate her sandwich.

"You're not looking. You're not laughing," Danny said.

"I'm eating," Beth told him. "That's why I'm here."

Danny took the bread off his nose and put it on his chin.

"Look now," he said. "I have a beard. I'm Abraham Lincoln."

"Danny, why don't you just eat your lunch," Beth said. She showed Danny his heart-shaped cookie. "Look at what your mother wrote on your dessert."

I Love You was written in red icing across the front of the cookie.

"That's because it's Valentine's Day," Danny said. "She always gives me heart cookies on Valentine's Day."

Beth told him, "Your mother wants you to eat your lunch."

"And I want to *wear* my lunch," Danny said.

When Danny spoke, the bread on his chin went up and down. Children at the next table laughed.

"Don't laugh," Beth told them. "If you laugh when he's silly, he gets sillier."

Danny did get sillier. He stood on his chair and made chicken noises.

"Cluck! Cluck! Cluck!"

He held up his apple and said, "I laid a red egg." He hugged it and said, "My little baby."

The children at the next table didn't laugh.

"You're right," a boy said. "He did get sillier."

Danny looked at the children at the next table. They were eating. He looked at Cam, Eric, and Beth. They were eating, too. Danny sat down. He took the bread off his chin and bit into it.

"Your mother is nice," Eric said to Danny. "She's a reading teacher," he told Cam and Beth. "In first grade, when I was having trouble learning to read, she helped me."

"Cam," Beth said. "How is *your* mother? When will she have the baby?"

"Soon, I think," Cam answered. "Maybe in a few weeks. She said I'll be surprised."

"What's the surprise?" Eric asked. "You know you're getting a sister."

"Maybe the surprise is, she'll be like Cam,"

Danny said. "She'll have a picture memory, too. She'll be born holding a camera. Instead of crying *'Boo hoo,'* she'll cry, *'Click! Click!'*"

Cam has an amazing photographic memory. It's as if she has pictures of whatever she's seen stored in her head. Whenever she wants to be sure she remembers something, she looks at it, blinks her eyes, and says, *"Click!"* Cam says that's the sound her mental camera makes when it takes a picture. When Cam wants to remember something she's seen, she says, *"Click!"* again.

Cam's real name is Jennifer Jansen, but when people found out about her amazing memory they started calling her, "The Camera." Soon "The Camera" became just "Cam."

Danny said, "We can call your new sister *Film* Jansen or *Flash* Jansen or *Click* Jansen."

Cam said, "I like the name Alice. It means 'truth.'"

Cam, Eric, and Beth had finished eating their lunches. They put the wrappers from their sandwiches and their empty milk containers in their lunch bags and threw them away.

"Hurry," Beth told Danny. "Lunchtime is almost over."

Danny took a big bite of his apple. Before he chewed it, he took a big bite of his heart-shaped cookie. His mouth was full. As he chewed the apple and cookie, crumbs fell onto the table.

Rrrr! Rrrr!

"That's the bell," Beth said. "Let's go."

Cam, Eric, and Beth started to leave the lunchroom.

"Wghmt aw we!" Danny said.

"What?" Beth asked.

Cam told her, "I think he said, 'Wait for me.'"

Danny threw away his wrappers. He wiped the cream cheese and jelly off his face with his sleeve and said, "I'm ready."

They left the lunchroom and walked toward their classroom.

The halls were decorated with large paper

hearts. In the middle of each heart was a message. Among them were, *I Love to Learn, I Love to Read,* and *I Love School.*

The children turned the corner. Their classroom was straight ahead, at the very end of the hall.

"Hey," Cam said. "Someone is talking to Ms. Benson."

"Maybe it's your mother," Beth said to Danny. "Maybe you're in trouble."

"No," Danny said as they got closer. "It's Eric's mother."

CHAPTER TWO

Eric ran to his mother.

"Why are you here, Mom? Is something wrong?"

"I came for Cam," Mrs. Shelton said. "Her mother is about to have the baby."

Ms. Benson told Eric, "Your mother is taking Cam to the hospital, so she can be there when her sister is born."

Cam, Beth, and Danny were by the door to the classroom now. Ms. Benson told Cam the good news. She told her to get her coat and books and go with Mrs. Shelton.

"I want to go, too," Eric said.

"You know, Eric is Cam's very best friend," Mrs. Shelton said. "It would be nice for both of them if he could go, too."

Ms. Benson smiled and said, "Eric may go."

"What about me?" Danny asked. "I'm also Cam's friend."

"I can't just let you leave school," Ms. Benson said. "I'll need a note from your mother or father."

Cam and Eric put on their coats. They gathered their books. They were ready to leave the classroom when Danny called out, "Wait for me!"

He gave Ms. Benson a note.

"This must be one of your jokes," Ms. Benson said after she read the note.

"It's not a joke," Danny said. "I want to go with Cam and Eric."

Ms. Benson read the note aloud. "'Please let me go to the *hapistal*.' That's what you wrote: '*hapistal*.' And you signed it, 'Danny's dad.'"

Danny smiled at Ms. Benson. She smiled, too, and shook her head. She wouldn't allow him to go with Cam and Eric.

Danny turned and started toward his seat, and children in the class laughed.

"What?" Danny asked. "I didn't even tell a joke."

Math worksheets from Ms. Benson's desk were stuck to the cream cheese and jelly on Danny's sleeve.

"That's a good idea," Ms. Benson said. "You can hand out the worksheets."

Danny went back to Ms. Benson's desk. He took the rest of the worksheets from her desk. He gave sheets to Cam and Eric. Then he walked through the room and gave one to each of his classmates.

Cam and Eric followed Mrs. Shelton to her car. "Buckle up," Mrs. Shelton said as they got in.

Cam and Eric got into the backseat of the car and put on their seat belts.

"What's the name of a triangle with all three sides the same length?" Eric asked. He was reading from the worksheet.

"I'm not thinking about triangles," Cam answered. "I'm thinking about my sister."

"That's exactly what I'm thinking about," Mrs. Shelton said. "Babies are so cute."

"It's equilateral," Eric said. Then he folded the worksheet. He put it in his jacket pocket and said, "I'll do this later."

It was a short ride to the hospital. Mrs. Shelton drove to the entrance of the parking garage. The gate was down. Mrs. Shelton stopped the car and pulled a ticket from the machine, and the gate went up.

"Here," Mrs. Shelton said, and gave Eric the ticket. "Please hold this."

It was a large garage with several levels. Mrs. Shelton drove along the ramps from one level to the next. The first empty spot she found was on the fifth level. Mrs. Shelton parked her car. When she, Cam, and Eric got out, she pushed the car clicker on her key ring. The car lights blinked as the doors locked.

"Let's go," Mrs. Shelton said.

The front lobby of the hospital was decorated with pink ribbons and lots of paper hearts.

"Hey," Eric told Cam. "Your sister's birthday will be February fourteenth, Valentine's Day. That's so great!"

Mrs. Shelton told the man at the front desk, "We're here to see Mrs. Jane Jansen."

"Maternity, fourth floor," the man said after he checked on the computer. Then he looked at Cam and Eric. "Are these Jane Jansen's children?"

"She's Mrs. Jansen's daughter, and he's my son."

The man smiled and said, "Go ahead upstairs."

Cam, Eric, and Mrs. Shelton went to the elevator. They got off at the fourth floor and followed signs to the maternity ward.

"Look, Cam," Mrs. Shelton said, and pointed down the hall. "There's your dad."

Cam ran to him.

He hugged Cam. "Mom is waiting to go to the delivery room," he said. "I'll tell her you're here." Then he hurried off.

CHAPTER THREE

"Babies have their own schedules," Mrs. Shelton said as she, Cam, and Eric went to the waiting room. "It may be a few minutes or a few hours before your sister is born."

In a large chair in the corner of the room was a man. His legs were stretched out onto a small table. His coat was over his legs, and he was asleep. A white-haired old woman and one with blonde hair were also in the room. They were sitting together and reading magazines. In the back of the room were vending machines, one with coffee and one with juice.

"It's hot here," Mrs. Shelton said, and took off her coat. She put the coat and her purse on a couch near the sleeping man. Cam and Eric also took off their coats.

Eric said, "Let's play a game while we wait. Let's play Geography. I'll name a place, like 'Texas.' That ends with an 'S.' Then you'll name a place that starts with an 'S,' like 'South Dakota.'"

"Let's do it with babies' names," Cam suggested, "and I'll go first." Then Cam smiled and said, "Alice."

"That ends with an 'E,'" Eric said. "Etain."

"Hey, that's a boy's name. I'm not having a brother."

"'Etain' is a name," Eric said, "and it ends with an 'N.'"

"'Nancy.'"

"'Y,'" Eric said. He thought for a moment and then said, "'Yale.'"

"'Ellen.'"

"'Nathan.'"

"'Naomi.'"

A man in a white doctor's jacket walked into the room.

"Maybe he's your mother's doctor," Mrs. Shelton said to Cam.

Mrs. Shelton quickly walked to the man. Cam and Eric followed her.

"Excuse me, Doctor," Mrs. Shelton said. "Can you tell me about Jane Jansen? How is she? Was she taken to the delivery room?"

"Jane Jansen," the man said, and rubbed his chin. "I don't think she's one of my patients."

"She has red hair," Mrs. Shelton said. "She's about to have a baby."

Just then a woman in a white doctor's coat walked into the waiting room.

"Maybe she can help you," the man said, and walked toward the coffee machine.

Cam, Eric, and Mrs. Shelton went to the woman.

The woman wore a name tag. Her name was Judith Berger.

"Please, Dr. Berger," Mrs. Shelton said, "can you tell us about Jane Jansen? How is she? Did she have her baby?"

Dr. Berger smiled. "I was just with Mrs. Jansen," she said, "and she's doing very well. It will be a while before I can tell you any more than that."

Dr. Berger went to the coffee machine.

Cam, Eric, and Mrs. Shelton went back to their seats.

"It's your turn," Cam told Eric. "I said 'Naomi' and that ends with an 'I.'"

"'Ian.'"

"'Nellie.'"

"I'm getting a cup of coffee," Mrs. Shelton told Cam and Eric. "Are you thirsty? Would you like some juice?"

Cam and Eric wanted orange juice.

Mrs. Shelton looked on the couch. She lifted her coat. Then she lifted Cam's and Eric's coats. "Hey," she said. "Where's my purse?"

CHAPTER FOUR

"Maybe it fell behind the couch," Eric said.

Cam and Eric crawled on the floor, first under and then behind the couch. They crawled out again holding a few candy wrappers and a dirty coffee cup.

"Look at both of you," Mrs. Shelton said. "Your hands and pants are filthy."

Eric wiped his hands on the seat of his pants and said, "They should keep this place cleaner. It's a hospital."

"Here," Mrs. Shelton said, and took two wrapped Wet Wipes from her coat pocket. "Please clean your hands."

Cam and Eric each tore one open and cleaned their hands.

Eric looked at the others in the waiting room. Dr. Berger was in the back, drinking coffee. The two old women were still reading, and the man in the corner was still asleep.

"Maybe he's not really asleep," Eric whispered. "Maybe he took Mom's purse and he hid it under his coat."

Eric quietly moved closer to the man. Eric smiled. The man didn't react. Eric stuck out his tongue and waved his hands. The man still didn't move.

The two old women had put down their magazines. They were standing next to Mrs. Shelton.

"What is he doing?" the white-haired woman asked.

"He wants to see if the man is sleeping," Cam whispered.

"What did you say?" the woman asked.

She had her hand cupped behind her ear.

"The boy wants to see if that man is sleeping," the blonde-haired woman said really loudly.

"That's the big problem in hospitals," the white-haired woman said. "People here always want to know if you're sleeping. I was a patient here once and I was sleeping and a nurse shook me. 'Are you sleeping?' she asked. 'Yes,' I said. 'Oh,' she told me, 'then you won't need this pill.' It was a pill to help me sleep. 'Well,' I told her, 'I need it now!'"

The man opened his eyes. All the loud talk had wakened him.

"We're looking for my mother's purse," Eric said.

The man rubbed his eyes.

"Did you see it?" Eric asked.

"My eyes were closed. I was asleep," the man said, and sat up. "I didn't see anything."

When he sat up, his coat fell onto the floor. Mrs. Shelton's purse wasn't by his legs. Eric bent to pick up the man's coat. When he did, he looked under the couch. The purse wasn't there.

"Thank you," the man said when Eric gave him his coat.

Eric went back to his seat. He pushed his coat aside and sat down. His mother and Cam sat beside him.

"Are you sure you had it with you?" Eric asked. "Maybe you left it in the car."

"I think I had it."

Cam closed her eyes. She said, *"Click!"* and looked at the picture she had in her head of Mrs. Shelton when she walked into the hospital.

"It's a green bag," Cam said with her eyes still closed.

"Yes," Mrs. Shelton said. "It matches my coat."

"You carried it over your left arm."

"When you came into this room you said, 'It's hot here,'" Eric said. "You put your purse on the couch, and then you took off your coat." Eric smiled, and said, "I have a good memory, too."

Cam opened her eyes. She looked around the waiting room at the man and the couch and the two old women and said, "They didn't take the purse."

"The only other people in here were the two doctors," Eric said, "Dr. Berger and the man."

"That's strange," Mrs. Shelton said. "We know Dr. Berger's name, but not the other doctor's."

Cam closed her eyes again and said, *"Click!"*

"Dr. Berger wore a hospital tag," Cam

said with her eyes still closed. "It had her name, Judith Berger, MD. But the other doctor had no tag."

"He said your mom was not one of his patients," Mrs. Shelton remembered.

"If he's a doctor, he should have a tag," Eric said.

Cam opened her eyes.

"He must be a fake," Cam told Mrs. Shelton, "and while we were talking to Dr. Berger, he stole your purse."

"Now what do we do?" Mrs. Shelton asked.

"We look for him," Cam said. "When we find the fake doctor, we'll find your purse."

"I'll call security," Mrs. Shelton said.

There was a telephone by the door. She lifted the handset, pushed a few buttons, and said, "I need to report a robbery."

CHAPTER FIVE

"Yes," Mrs. Shelton said into the telephone handset. "I can describe the thief." She thought for a moment. "He has blond hair and is wearing a white doctor's jacket, and . . . and . . . and that's about all I remember. Oh, and he has my purse. It's big and green."

"Wait," Cam said. "I remember more."

Cam closed her eyes and said, *"Click!"* Then, with her eyes still closed, she described the man to Mrs. Shelton.

"He has a round face, curly blond hair, blue eyes, and a small scratch on his right cheek, and he's wearing a silver ring with a blue stone on the middle finger of his right hand."

Mrs. Shelton repeated Cam's description to the security guard. She listened for a moment and then put the telephone handset back on its cradle.

"The security guards will look for him," she said, "and they'll call the police."

Cam opened her eyes.

"What about us?" Eric asked. "What should we do?"

"We can look, too," Mrs. Shelton said. "We'll look for my purse. Maybe the thief dropped it. But if we see the thief, we won't say or do anything. He could be dangerous. We'll just come back here and call security."

Cam, Eric, and Mrs. Shelton left the waiting room. Mrs. Shelton went directly to the nurse's station. She told the nurse about the fake doctor.

"I still have my cell phone," she told the nurse. It was in a holder on her waist. She gave the nurse her cell phone number and said, "We won't be in the waiting room, but we want to know just as soon as you have any news about Jane Jansen."

"Don't worry. I'll call you just as soon as she's taken to the delivery room," the nurse said. "And I hope you find your purse."

Cam, Eric, and Mrs. Shelton walked down the hall. A man wearing a white jacket hurried past, but he had long dark hair and a name tag. A man in a white jacket came out of an office, but he didn't have blond

hair. He had no hair. He was bald. Then two men in white jackets got off the elevator. Neither was the fake doctor.

"Oh!" Eric said, and threw up his hands. "They all wear white jackets and none of them is the thief!"

"Maybe he went downstairs," Cam said when they reached the elevator. "Maybe he left the building."

"All my credit cards are in my purse," Mrs. Shelton said, "and my driver's license, library card, and medical insurance card. First I'll have to cancel all those cards. Then I'll have to replace them. There's money and keys in my purse. This is terrible."

"Don't worry," Eric told his mother. "Cam will find your purse."

But how will I find it? Cam wondered. Then she had an idea.

"What would you do if you were the thief?" she asked Eric. "What would you do if you had just stolen someone's purse?"

"I would never steal," Eric answered.

"Please," Cam said. "Help me with this. Pretend you're a thief."

Eric folded his arms and looked up at the ceiling. Then he shook his head and told Cam, "I'm sorry. I can't."

"Well, I can," Cam said. "The thief must know people will be looking for a man in a white jacket carrying your mom's green purse. First he would take off the jacket. Then he'd empty the purse, get rid of it, and run."

Cam looked up and down the hall and asked, "Where would he leave the jacket and purse?"

"I'd throw it in a trash can," Mrs. Shelton said, and went to the nearest one. She took off the lid. She looked in, moved some papers, and said, "It's not in here, but there are lots more trash cans."

Mrs. Shelton went to the next one and lifted the lid.

"Yuck!" she said.

Cam and Eric looked in.

It was filled with papers, bread, tuna fish, and tomato juice.

"Someone didn't like his lunch," Mrs. Shelton said.

She carefully pushed aside some papers but didn't find the white jacket and green purse.

"I've been trying to do what you said and think like a thief," Eric told Cam. "I don't think a thief would want someone to see him throw good things away. He'd go where no one would see, and then get rid of the stuff."

"You're right," Cam said. "Let's look for an empty room or a stairway."

"We didn't pass any empty rooms," Mrs. Shelton said, "but there's a door marked *Stairs* just across from the elevator."

Cam, Eric, and Mrs. Shelton hurried to the stairs. They opened the door, and on the floor were a white jacket and an open green purse.

"Oh," Mrs. Shelton said as she took her purse. "I'm so glad we found it."

Eric smiled and said, "I knew Cam would solve this mystery."

"Nothing is solved," Cam told Eric. "We have to see what was stolen from your mom's purse. Then we have to help security catch the thief."

CHAPTER SIX

Mrs. Shelton opened her purse. She took out her wallet and found all her credit cards and driver's license. Then she opened her billfold and said, "My money is gone."

"Please, keep looking," Cam told her. "Maybe he took something else."

Mrs. Shelton took a tube of lipstick, hand cream, and toothpaste from her purse. She gave them to Eric to hold. Then she took out a can opener, two pens, a shoehorn, a box of raisins, an envelope filled with coupons, and a pack of chewing gum.

"It's all here," Mrs. Shelton said. "He

took my money, but nothing else."

"What about your keys?" Cam asked.

Mrs. Shelton looked in her purse again.

"They're gone," she said. "He took my money *and* my keys!"

Ring! Ring!

Mrs. Shelton took her cell phone from the holder on her waist.

"Hello."

She listened.

"Yes," Mrs. Shelton said. "We'll be right there."

Mrs. Shelton quickly left the stairwell. Then she turned and called to Cam and Eric, "Let's go! Let's go! Cam's mom is having the baby!"

"What did she say?" Cam asked as they hurried down the hall.

"Your mom was taken to the delivery room. The nurse said we should go to the waiting room and wait there. Someone will come in and tell us as soon as your sister is born."

Mrs. Shelton pushed open the door to the waiting room. The man was still asleep on the large chair in the corner. The two old women were still reading magazines.

"How long do we have to wait?" Cam asked.

Mrs. Shelton smiled. "The only one who might know that is your sister, and she's not talking."

"She probably won't be talking for a long time," Eric said. "She'll just cry and wake you up at night."

"I'm going to teach her to talk," Cam said. "I'll hold her, talk to her, and read her my favorite books."

Eric said, "You can teach her to say *'Click!'*"

Cam smiled. "First I'll teach her to say 'Mama' and 'Papa' and 'Cam-Cam.'"

Just then the door opened. Dr. Berger came in and told Mrs. Shelton, "I have good news. It's a strong, healthy boy."

"Are you sure it's a boy?" Mrs. Shelton asked.

"I'm a doctor. I know the difference between a boy and a girl."

"But I'm having a sister," Cam said.

"Are you the Normans?"

"No," Cam said. "I'm Jennifer Jansen."

"Oh, where are the Normans?"

"We're right here," the blonde woman said.

The two women put down their magazines and went to Dr. Berger.

"I'm Mildred Norman," the blonde woman said. "I'm the baby's grandmother."

"And I'm Betty Walters," the other woman told Dr. Berger. "I'm his grandmother, too."

"He is beautiful. In a few minutes you can see him. He'll be in the nursery."

"How is my daughter?" Mrs. Walters asked.

"She's fine, just a little tired."

The two women left the waiting room. Dr. Berger was about to follow them when Mrs. Shelton stopped her and asked, "How is Jane Jansen?"

"She's in the delivery room," Dr. Berger said on her way out, "but I don't know when she'll have her babies."

Just then Mildred Norman hurried back into the room.

"I forgot my camera," she said, and grabbed a bag she had left on her seat. "I brought it here to take pictures of the baby, and I forgot it."

"Yes!" Cam said. "People take things for a reason."

"Of course we do," Mildred Norman said.

"He's just so beautiful. I plan to take lots of pictures of him. That's why I brought my camera."

Mildred Norman left the waiting room.

Cam went to the window and looked out. "I hope it's not too late," she said, "but I think I know how to catch the thief. We have to call the security guards."

Mrs. Shelton picked up the telephone handset. She started to press the buttons. Then she stopped.

"What do I tell them?" she asked.

"People take things for a reason," Cam explained. "The thief took your money because he wants to spend it. He took your car keys because he wants to use them."

"But he doesn't know where to find my car."

"Yes he does. It's where all the people here park their cars. It's in the hospital parking garage."

CHAPTER SEVEN

Mrs. Shelton smiled. "He can't steal my car," she said. "He won't know which one it is."

"He doesn't have to know," Cam said. "He'll just push the clicker and see which car's lights blink."

"Oh, you're right. What do we do?"

"We call the guards."

Mrs. Shelton picked up the telephone handset again and called the security guards. "I'm calling about my stolen purse."

She listened for a moment and then said, "Yes, I'll wait."

"We can't wait," Cam said. "The thief is getting away!"

Cam rushed out of the room. Mrs. Shelton put down the telephone. Then she and Eric followed Cam.

"Where are we going?" Eric asked.

"Downstairs," Cam said. "We'll tell the guards to go to the parking garage and look for the thief."

Cam pressed the button for the elevator.

"The police are here," Mrs. Shelton said. "That's why the guard told me to wait."

"Good," Cam said as the elevator door opened. "We'll talk to the police. Maybe they can catch the thief."

Cam pressed the button for the main floor. She waited. When the doors didn't close, she pressed the button again. She was in a hurry.

The doors closed. The elevator was on its way down.

"You can describe the thief," Eric said.

"And I'll describe my car," Mrs. Shelton added.

The elevator stopped on the second floor. Cam, Eric, and Mrs. Shelton moved to the back of the elevator as a young man pushed on a woman in a wheelchair.

Cam tapped her foot.

"Hello," the man said, and pressed the button for the main floor. "I'm Bob and this is Gail."

Cam squeezed past the wheelchair and pressed the button a few times.

"We're in a hurry," Cam explained as the doors closed.

"You should never hurry," Bob said.

"That's right," Gail added. "I hurried and crashed into a telephone pole."

"Her car was ruined," the man said, "but Gail is fine now."

The elevator doors opened. Bob slowly wheeled Gail out. Cam, Eric, and Mrs. Shelton followed them.

"There they are," Cam said. She pointed to a security guard and two police officers who were by the hospital entrance. Cam ran to them.

"Don't run!" Bob called out. "Don't run!"

Eric and his mother slowly followed Cam.

"The thief," Cam told the police officers and security guard, "the one who stole the purse, may be in the parking garage."

"I think she's right," Mrs. Shelton said. She told them about the keys and the clicker. Then she described her car. "The car is on the fifth level, so it will take him time to find it."

"But once he does," the officer said, "he

just drives to the exit, takes the ticket off the dashboard, pays the parking fee, and drives off."

"Oh, no," Eric said. "I have the ticket."

Eric took the ticket from his pocket and showed it to the police officers and the guard.

"That's great! He'll have to fill out a lost ticket form," the security guard said, "and that will take a while."

The two police officers quickly left the hospital and walked toward the parking garage. The guard took the walkie-talkie off her

belt and called the garage attendant. She told him about Mrs. Shelton's car.

"He just left!" the guard said. Then she quickly returned her walkie-talkie to her belt clip and ran out of the hospital.

Cam, Eric, and Mrs. Shelton went to the large window and looked out.

"There's my car!" Mrs. Shelton said.

Her car was leaving the parking garage. The guard caught up to the police officers. She pointed to Mrs. Shelton's car. The officers got into their car and turned on the siren.

Rrrr! Rrrr!

The police sped off after the thief.

Ring! Ring!

"Mom," Eric said. "It's your cell phone. It's ringing."

Mrs. Shelton pressed a button and spoke into her cell phone. "Hello," she said, and listened. Then she asked, "Are you sure?"

She put the phone back on her waist clip.

"It was the woman at the nurse's station,"

she told Cam. "She said your *brother* was born. I think she mixed us up with the Normans again."

"Maybe she didn't mix us up," Cam said. "Maybe my parents were wrong when they told me I was getting a sister."

Cam, Eric, and Mrs. Shelton took the elevator to the fourth floor. The doors opened and Mr. Jansen was standing there, waiting for Cam.

"It's a boy," he said. "He was born first. And a girl. Mom had twins!"

"Wow! That's double great!" Cam said. "That's why Dr. Berger told us she didn't know when Mom would have her *babies*. She said 'babies' because she knew Mom was having twins."

"We knew it, too," Cam's father said. "You asked Mom if you would be getting a sister and she said, 'Yes.'"

"And you said I would be surprised."

"Are you?"

"Yes!" Cam said and hugged her dad. "I'm more than surprised. I'm so very happy."

CHAPTER EIGHT

Cam and her father and Eric and his mother all went to the nursery. They stood behind a large window and looked in at a room full of newborn babies, each in a small bassinet. On the side of each bassinet was a card with the baby's name.

"There they are," Mr. Jansen said, and pointed to the back of the nursery.

"They're tiny," Cam said. "But they're beautiful."

Cam pressed close to the window, but she couldn't read the cards with their names.

Mr. Jansen waved to the two nurses in the back of the nursery. He pointed to the twins and then to himself, so they would know he was their father. The nurses smiled and wheeled the bassinets closer.

"Oh, they're adorable," Mrs. Shelton said.

"Seth," Cam said, "and Alice. I like those names."

"Mom and I like them, too," Mr. Jansen said.

Cam looked at Seth and Alice Jansen. Her brother and sister looked to her like

two perfect dolls. It was hard for Cam to imagine that she had once been that small or that one day they would be as big as she was now.

Cam and the others watched the babies for a long time. Then Mr. Jansen said, "Let's visit Mom."

They all walked down a long hall to the room Cam's mom shared with another new mother. When they walked into the room, Mrs. Jansen put her finger to her lips and pointed to the woman in the next bed. She was sleeping.

Mrs. Jansen reached out and took Cam's hand. She held it and smiled. It was a happy, tired smile.

"The babies are beautiful," Cam whispered. "I like their names, and it's so great they're twins."

They all stood there for a while and whispered about Cam's new brother and sister.

"Mom is tired," Mr. Jansen whispered. "I think we should go now."

Once they were outside the room, Cam's father thanked Mrs. Shelton for bringing Cam to the hospital. Then he asked, "Could you take Cam home? I'll pick her up at your house when I get back."

"Of course I can. Oh! Maybe I can't."

Mrs. Shelton told Cam's father about her stolen purse. "Then, just before the nurse called, we saw the thief drive off with my car."

They all walked to the elevator. "I'll go downstairs with you," Mr. Jansen said. "If you don't get your car back, I'll drive you home."

"I'll help you and Mom with the twins," Cam told her father in the elevator. "I'll read to them and feed them and play with them."

"And change their diapers," Eric added.

Cam made a face. She wasn't sure she wanted to change Seth's and Alice's diapers.

"Mom and I would like you to help," Mr. Jansen said. "But only after you finish your schoolwork."

The elevator doors opened.

"There they are!" Danny shouted.

Danny, Beth, and Ms. Benson were near the reception desk.

Danny told Cam, "My dad said Ms. Benson could take me here after school."

"Was your sister born? Is she pretty? What's her name and how is your mom?" Beth asked.

"Yes, yes, Alice and Mom are fine, but Mom is tired," Cam answered.

"That's wonderful," Ms. Benson said.

Cam smiled. "Aren't you going to ask about my brother?"

"What brother?" Danny asked.

"Cam's mom had twins!" Eric shouted.

"Shhh," Ms. Benson said. "This is a hospital."

"Their names are Seth and Alice," Cam whispered.

"That's so nice," Ms. Benson said. "And they picked Valentine's Day to be born. That's so sweet."

"Hey," Danny said. "Here's a baby riddle.

Who is smarter, Mrs. Smarter or Mrs. Smarter's baby?"

"Excuse me," Mrs. Shelton said, and went over to speak to the security guard.

"Mom's purse and car were stolen," Eric said. "We even saw the thief drive off with her car."

"Wow!" Beth said. "You really had an exciting day. All I did was learn about triangles, rivers, and poetry."

Then Beth turned and saw Ms. Benson.

"Oops!"

"That's okay," Ms. Benson said. "Cam *did* have an exciting day."

"Cam solved the mystery of who stole Mom's purse," Eric said. "She told the police where to find the thief."

"Look," Mrs. Shelton said. She held her keys out as she walked over. "They caught the thief. Mine was the third car this week that was stolen from the hospital parking lot. The police think this man stole all three. Now my car is in the parking lot. I'll get my

money back, too, but first I have to go to the police station and fill out a report." Mrs. Shelton smiled and said, "Thank you, Cam."

"Really," Danny said. "Who is smarter?"

"Do you want to see Seth and Alice?" Mr. Jansen asked Ms. Benson.

"Of course I do."

"It's the baby," Danny said. "The baby is a little Smarter."

No one laughed.

"Don't you get it? The baby is little and its

last name is Smarter, so it's a little Smarter."

"You're not funny," Beth told him.

"Oh yes I am," he said.

Mr. Jansen spoke with the man at the front desk. Then he told Ms. Benson that she could go up and see the babies. Danny and Beth would have to wait in the lobby with him.

"Good-bye," Cam said to Danny, Beth, and Ms. Benson. Then she went with Eric and Mrs. Shelton to the garage.

Mrs. Shelton said, "I wonder where my car is parked."

"Please, Mom," Eric said. "Give me your keys and I'll do what Cam said. I'll pretend I'm the thief."

She gave Eric the keys. He hurried ahead. He held the keys over his head and pressed the clicker. He was looking for a car with blinking lights.

Eric had hurried right past a car parked by the entrance to the garage. It was his mother's car.

Cam laughed and told Mrs. Shelton, "Eric doesn't make a very good thief."

"I'm glad he doesn't," his mother said. "But he is a very good son."

"And a very good friend," Cam added.

Cam called to Eric and pointed to the car. Then they drove home together, happily talking about Cam's new brother and sister, Seth and Alice Jansen.

A Cam Jansen Memory Game

Take another look at the picture opposite page 1. Study it. Blink your eyes and say, *"Click!"* Then turn back to this page and answer these questions. Please, first study the picture, *then* look at the questions.

1. What is Danny, the boy sitting next to Eric, doing?
2. Who is Cam sitting next to?
3. How many children are sitting at the table?
4. Is it a round table or a square table?
5. What shapes are taped to the lunch-room windows?
6. Is there an adult in the picture?

Super Memory Question:
How many apples are on the table?

Cam Jansen

25th Anniversary

Memory Quizzes & Trivia Questions

Cam Jansen has a
photographic memory. Do *you?*
Look back over twenty-five years
of Cam Jansen mysteries to see
how much you remember.

Cam Jansen

Memory Quizzes!

Study the following pictures.
As you look at each one,
blink your eyes and say, *"Click!"*
Then turn to the questions for that
picture and try to answer them.
When you are done, look back at the
pictures and see how you did.

Cam Jansen and the Mystery of the Stolen Diamonds, #1

Cam Jansen and the Mystery of the Babe Ruth Baseball, #6

Cam Jansen and the Mystery at the Monkey House, #10

Cam Jansen and the
Scary Snake Mystery, #17

Cam Jansen
and the
Mystery of the Stolen
Diamonds, #1

Memory Quiz Questions:

1. Who is standing on the bench?
2. Is the running man fat or thin?
3. Does he have a mustache or beard?
4. Is he wearing a striped shirt?
5. Which direction is the man running?
6. Is anyone wearing a hat?

Super Memory Question:

What's the name of the jewelry store?

Cam Jansen
and the
Mystery of the
Babe Ruth Baseball, #6

Memory Quiz Questions:

1. Who is pointing at the Babe Ruth sign?
2. Is Eric wearing a baseball cap?
3. Who is standing next to Eric?
4. Is anyone sitting by the Babe Ruth display?
5. What's the name of the coin shop that has a display at the hobby show?
6. What's on the raised stand at the very front of the picture?

Super Memory Question:
How many cuckoo clocks are on the back wall?

Cam Jansen
and the
Mystery at the
Monkey House, #10

Memory Quiz Questions:

1. How many people are in the picture?
2. How many are standing on their hands?
3. What is the letter on the boy's hat?
4. Are any monkeys playing on the swings?
5. Is Cam looking at the monkeys?
6. Is anyone wearing a short-sleeved shirt?

Super Memory Question:
How many monkeys are in the picture?

Cam Jansen

and the
Scary Snake Mystery, #17

Memory Quiz Questions:

1. What is the man pointing at?
2. Is he wearing a jacket?
3. Does he look happy?
4. Is Cam standing? Is Eric?
5. Is the woman with the camera wearing a skirt or pants?

Super Memory Question:

What's Eric wearing, pants or shorts?

The Cam Jansen Twenty-Fifth Anniversary Trivia Quiz

(Answers on page 74)

1. "Cam" is Cam Jansen's nickname. What is her real first name?

    A. Jessica   C. Jennifer

    B. Stephanie   D. Betty

2. "Cam" is short for

    A. Camellia   C. Caramel

    B. The Camera D. Camel

3. Cam remembers just about everything she

    A. hears   C. sees

    B. reads   D. learns

4. What does Cam say when she wants to remember something?

    A. *"Clock!"*   C. *"Cluck!"*

    B. *"Click!"*   D. *"Hello."*

5. We first meet Cam Jansen's classroom teacher in *Cam Jansen and the Mystery of the Dinosaur Bones* (#3). What's her name?

    A. Ms. Adams   C. Ms. Green

    B. Ms. Baker   D. Ms. Benson

6. What color is Cam's hair?

    A. Red   C. Black

    B. Blonde   D. Brown

7. What is Eric's last name?

    A. Smith   C. Rivers

    B. Shelton   D. Jones

8. We meet Eric's twin sisters in *Cam Jansen and the Mystery of the Television Dog* (#4). What are their names?

    A. Jane and June

    B. Donna and Diane

C. Candy and Cindy

D. Francine and Felice

9. What is the television dog's name?
   A. Cloudy   C. Poochie
   B. Rover   D. Fido

10. We first meet Cam's funny aunt Molly in *Cam Jansen and the Mystery of the Circus Clown* (#7). Molly travels a lot because she works for
   A. the circus   C. a bus company
   B. an airline   D. a baseball team

11. What has never been stolen in any Cam Jansen mystery?
   A. Diamonds   C. Computers
   B. A gold watch   D. A corn popper

12. We learn Cam's parents' first names in *Cam Jansen and the Birthday Mystery* (#20). What are their first names?
   A. Anne and David
   B. Joseph and Arlene

C. Barbara and Elliot

D. Jane and Barry

13. What's the "barking treasure" in *Cam Jansen and the Barking Treasure Mystery* (#19)?

   A. A seal   C. A puppet

   B. A dog   D. A game

14. What's the name of the movie Cam and Eric watch in *Cam Jansen and the Mystery of the Monster Movie* (#8)?

   A. *Revenge of the Ten-Foot Spiders*

   B. *Prince Paws*

   C. *Shoe Escape*

   D. *Gila Monster Madness*

15. Who in Cam's class loves to tell jokes?

   A. Beth   C. Susan

   B. Jacob   D. Danny

16. Cam's gym teacher is in several books. What's his name?

   A. Mr. Day   C. Mr. Davis

   B. Mr. Benson   D. Mr. Jackson

17. In *Cam Jansen and the Snowy Day Mystery* (#24), Mrs. Lane, the bus driver, says, "It's only snow! It's just tiny ____." Tiny what?

   A. things   C. drops

   B. flakes   D. particles

18. Who is arrested in *Cam Jansen and the First Day of School Mystery* (#22)?

   A. Cam's teacher

   B. Cam's friend Eric

   C. The school principal

   D. No one is arrested

Answers:

1. C
2. B
3. C
4. B
5. D
6. A
7. B
8. B
9. C
10. B
11. B
12. D
13. B
14. C
15. D
16. A
17. B
18. A